This

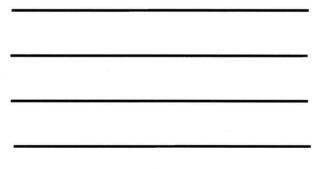

book belongs to

_____

_____

_____

_____

_____

27

bug

braincell

cat

rabbits

slug

jellyfish

frog

triCeratops

horse

cow

aardvark

bee

armadillo

amoeba

shark

elephant

sheep

snail

dog

bat

whale

stegosaurus

moose

hippo

puffin

pea brain

penguin

pig

hedgehog

zebra

tabbycat

tyrannosaurus rex

plankton

spider

duckbilledplatypus

To Sophie and Mark
love Jackie.
JR

To Jake
love Mummy.
KD

First published in 2000 by
David Bennett Books Limited
United Kingdom.

BRITISH LIBRARY CATALOGUING IN PUBLICATION DATA
A catalogue record for this book is available from the British Library.

ISBN 1-85602-384-2

Printed in Singapore

The story of
amoeba

Created by bang on the door™

Illustrated by
Karen Duncan and Samantha Stringle

Story by
Jackie Robb and Berny Stringle

David Bennett Books

Amoeba was a tiny blob
who lived beside the lake.

It was Amoeba's birthday
but he hadn't got a cake.

He didn't have a party,
or a present, or a card.

He was trying to be happy, but he found it very hard.

He wished his neighbours
would come by
to help him celebrate -

To say, "Congratulations"
or, "Happy birthday, mate!"

He even tried to get to know
the fish who lived around him,

But they were very snooty –
they just splashed him and
half-drowned him.

He searched every pond
and puddle
to find a fellow creature,

But no-one seemed to be about to say, "It's nice to meet ya!"

Now the Moon in a puddle
was just a reflection,

But he had the solution
to Amoeba's rejection.

"It's so easy for you
to make your own friend -

You just stretch yourself out
then split off at the end!"

"I can?!" asked Amoeba,
"Is that really true?"

"Just try it," said Moon,
"While you're at it, make two!"

The two got the giggles, saying, "Let's make some more."

They split their sides laughing
and then – there were four!

They did it again
and now there were eight.

"You all look like me!"
said Amoeba, "It's great!"

Amoeba was happy —
he had his own gang,

He knew that his party
would go with a bang.

No-one knew each other's name
and they all got in a muddle.

But they kept on multiplying as they partied in the puddle.

The Story of Amoeba
ISBN 1 85602 384-2

The Story of Armadillo
ISBN 1 85602 337-0

The Story of Bat
ISBN 1 85602 316-8

The Story of Brain Cell
ISBN 1 85602 319-2

The Story of Cat
ISBN 1 85602 314-1

The Story of Dog
ISBN 1 85602 315-X

The Story of Pea Brain
ISBN 1 85602 383-4

The Story of Plankton
ISBN 1 85602 336-2

The Story of Slug
ISBN 1 85602 317-6

The Story of Spider
ISBN 1 85602 318-4

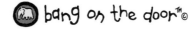 bang on the door™©

paperbacks are published by David Bennett Books
and available from all good bookshops.

dog

bat

whale

stegosaurus

moose

hippo

puffin

pea brain

penguin

pig

hedgehog

zebra

tabby cat

tyrannosaurus rex

plankton

spider

duck billed platypus